Bulldogs

Sarah Frank

Lerner Publications ◆ Minneapolis

Lerner Publications Company
A division of Lerner Publishing Group, Inc.
241 First Avenue North
Minneapolis, MN 55401 USA

For reading levels and more information, look up this title at www.lernerbooks.com.

Library of Congress Cataloging-in-Publication Data

The Cataloging-in-Publication Data for *Bulldogs* is on file at the Library of Congress.
ISBN 978-1-5415-5572-3 (lib. bdg.)
ISBN 978-1-5415-7464-9 (pbk.)
ISBN 978-1-5415-5662-1 (eb pdf)

Manufactured in the United States of America
2-1009729-43350-5/31/2023

Table of Contents

Quite a Pooch!

Bulldogs have their own special look. Some people giggle when they see these wrinkly pooches! But bulldog owners think their dogs are the best.

Bulldogs look like they mean business!

Bulldogs aren't very tall. Yet they weigh about 50 pounds (23 kg). These dogs are sturdy and strong.

Bulldogs have steady personalities. They love people. And they are great with kids and other animals.

Bulldogs want to be near their owners. They may weigh a lot. But they still want to sit on your lap. They give lots of big, wet kisses too.

Sturdy Bulldogs

The American Kennel Club (AKC) groups similar kinds of dogs together. The AKC puts bulldogs in the nonsporting group. Most nonsporting dogs are sturdy.

Bulldogs come from Britain.
People bred them to fight
bulls. But many dogs got hurt,
and Britain stopped the fights.

Bulls have
sharp horns.

Bulldogs are fun
to watch in shows.

The British started breeding
bulldogs to be in dog shows
instead. The dogs did well in
shows. They still do!

Bulldogs also make beloved pets. Their mild personalities help them fit in anywhere.

Bulldogs are very laid-back.

The Pet for You?

Bulldogs are great. But no one pet is right for every family. Decide with your family whether a bulldog is your perfect pet.

Bulldogs should be brushed a lot. Their wrinkles need cleaning too. Are you up for cleaning your dog's wrinkles with a wet cloth every day?

Don't get a bulldog if you don't have time to clean it.

Bulldogs tend to overheat. Can you keep your home at about 70°F (21°C)? Find out from a parent.

Bulldogs do best in cool weather.

Bulldogs often snore. Will this bother you? If you're a light sleeper, pass on a bulldog.

Is that snoring I hear?

Coming Home

If you still want a bulldog, you'll need a few supplies. Pick up a leash and bowls before your furry friend comes home.

Vets are doctors for animals.

Puppies and dogs need to go to the vet. Make a vet appointment for your dog right after she joins your family.

Your bulldog needs a good dog food. Ask your vet which food is best. A 50-pound (23 kg) bulldog needs about 1 pound (0.5 kg) of food a day.

Your bulldog will be a loyal pet. It will also be a great, goofy friend. You can count on this special dog to bring you miles of smiles.

Aw, BFFs!

Doggone Good Tips!

- Looking for a great name for your bulldog? Here are some you might like: Victor, Spike, Princess, Merlin, Boomer, or Earl.

- Bulldog puppies are fantastic, but full-grown bulldogs also make great pets. See if your local humane society has an adult bulldog you could adopt.

- Don't get a bulldog if you're looking for a watchdog. Bulldogs love to meet new people. Your bulldog may mistake a robber for its new best friend!

Why Bulldogs Are the Best

- No other dog looks quite like a bulldog. Get ready for lots of attention when you take your roly-poly bulldog for a walk.

- Many school teams pick bulldogs as mascots. Even the US Marines have a bulldog mascot.

- A bulldog named Spike has a role in the *Tom and Jerry* cartoon. Spike does not like cats. But he has a soft spot for mice. He's also very ticklish.

Glossary

American Kennel Club (AKC): an organization that groups dogs by breed

breed: to raise dogs for a special job or purpose. *Breed* can also mean "a certain type of dog."

loyal: having or showing support for someone

mild: gentle or calm

nonsporting group: a group of dogs that tend to be sturdy and come from a variety of backgrounds

sturdy: strong and healthy

vet: a doctor who treats animals

Further Reading

American Kennel Club
https://www.akc.org

American Society for the Prevention of Cruelty to Animals
https://www.aspca.org

Gray, Susan H. *Bulldogs*. New York: AV2 by Weigl, 2017.

Schuh, Mari. *The Supersmart Dog*. Minneapolis: Lerner Publications, 2019.

Statts, Leo. *Bulldogs*. Minneapolis: Abdo Zoom, 2017.

Index

Photo Acknowledgments

Image credits: ltummy/Shutterstock.com, pp. 2, 4; otsphoto/Shutterstock.com, p. 5; Twinkle Studio/Shutterstock.com, p. 6; WilleeCole Photography/Shutterstock.com, p. 7; badmanproduction/Getty Images, p. 8; Bipedbones/Shutterstock.com, p. 9; TIMOTHY A. CLARY/Staff/Getty Images, p. 10; WilleeCole Photography/Shutterstock.com, p. 11; Vadim Zakharishchev/Shutterstock.com, p. 12; ChasIKS/Shutterstock.com, p. 13; KAZLOVA IRYNA/Shutterstock.com, p. 14; Pond Thananat/Shutterstock.com, p. 15; Andrew Burgess/Shutterstock.com, p. 16; Luis Carlos Torres/Shutterstock.com, p. 16; LWA/Larry Williams/Getty Images, p. 17; Eric Isselee/Shutterstock.com, p. 18; David Fischer/Getty Images, p. 19; WilleeCole/Getty Images, p. 23.

Cover: Eric Isselee/Shutterstock.com.

Main body text set in Billy Infant regular 28/36. Typeface provided by SparkType.